Black Velvet

Black Beauty has been a favourite ever since
Anna Sewell wrote about him during the reign
of Queen Victoria.

Now, nearly a hundred years later, Josephine,
Diana and Christine Pullein-Thompson tell
the story of three descendants of the famous
horse in a trilogy called, collectively, BLACK
BEAUTY'S CLAN. Though BLACK VELVET
is chronologically the third story, each one
is quite complete in itself and can be enjoyed
even if you haven't read the other two books.

BLACK BEAUTY'S CLAN:
BLACK EBONY by Josephine Pullein-Thompson
BLACK PRINCESS by Diana Pullein-Thompson
BLACK VELVET by Christine Pullein-Thompson

*'I found these books difficult to put down. For
those of you who enjoyed Anna Sewell's classic,
I can wholeheartedly recommend them.'*
Pony Magazine

Anna Sewell's classic, BLACK BEAUTY, is
also available in Knight Books.

Foreword

BY BLACK ABBOT

Black Beauty's great-great-great-great nephew

Because of the world-wide interest shown in the autobiography of my kinsman, Black Beauty, I have now taken the liberty of gathering together the life stories written by three other members of my extraordinarily talented family.

These three mildewed manuscripts, the third of which, chronologically, is BLACK PRINCESS, were found in a loft, in a saddle room medicine cupboard and beneath a pile of rubbish in a deserted loosebox, and, except for the occasional indecipherable word, have been published exactly as they were written.

I have compiled a simple family tree to help those who wish to know the exact relationship each story-teller bears to our famous kinsman.

Black Velvet

Christine Pullein-Thompson

Illustrated by Elisabeth Grant

KNIGHT BOOKS
Hodder and Stoughton

Text copyright BLACK VELVET © 1975
Christine Pullein-Thompson

First published 1975 by the Brockhampton
Press Ltd., as one of the books in a
volume entitled BLACK BEAUTY'S CLAN

BLACK VELVET first published by
Knight Books 1979

Printed and bound in Great Britain for
Hodder and Stoughton Paperbacks, a
division of Hodder and Stoughton Ltd.,
Mill Road, Dunton Green, Sevenoaks,
Kent (Editorial Office: 47 Bedford
Square, London, WC1 3DP) by
Hunt Barnard Printing Ltd.,
Aylesbury, Bucks.

ISBN 0 340 23239 0

Contents

BLACK BEAUTY'S CLAN

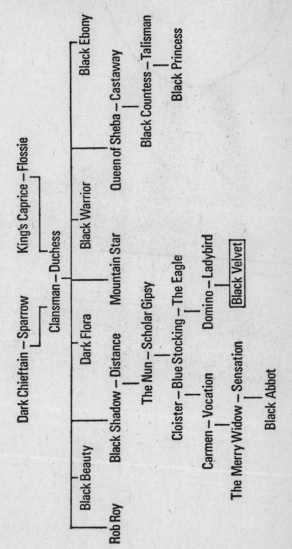

CHAPTER ONE

A fair beginning

I was born on a farm. It lay in a valley with gentle green hills on each side topped by tall trees. The fields were fenced by high hedges so there was always plenty of shelter from driving rain and clumps of trees gave us shade in summer.

My mother was dark brown with a beautiful head and a large, kind eye. Our master called her Ladybird and she was a great favourite with him. He rode her to hounds and about the farm. Sometimes on market days she pulled the high-wheeled trap.

There were five other horses on the farm, Merlin and Mermaid, the Shire horses, which pulled the plough and the wagon at harvest time. They were grey with huge fetlocks, and so large that even my mother, who was sixteen hands high, looked small and slender beside them. There was Rosie, a cheerful chestnut mare who did all the odd jobs, carting mangolds and kale to the cattle in winter, helping out when times were busy by pulling the harrow and the hay rake at harvest time. She was used on market days as well when the cart was needed instead of the trap. She did more work than any of the other horses on the farm, but I never heard her complain. Smallest of us all was Sinbad, the little piebald pony which our master's children rode, and who pulled the governess cart when our mistress went shopping or visiting friends.

We were a happy bunch of horses, well-fed and kindly treated. I was the youngest and came in for a good deal of teasing; but my mother always took my side, and I knew my master was proud of me for I heard him say once, 'You've really produced a good 'un this time Ladybird. He's the best looking colt I've seen for a long time.'

And though my mother told me I was wrong to listen to what was being said, she also told me that my father was one of the best looking horses in England.

'He's a relation of that great horse Black Beauty,' she said, 'and he's as black as you are, but with a star.'

It was a long time before I saw my father, but one day he came to the farm and stayed the night. My mother neighed with joy when she saw him. He was led by a small bandy legged man called 'a stallion walker' who slept near his loosebox. I was very proud when I saw my father. His coat shone like satin and he carried himself like a king. I neighed to him over the field gate, and he threw up his head and arched his beautiful neck and neighed back. That was the only time I ever saw him, for the next day he was led on to another farm, which was how he spent his life, moving from one farm to another all through the spring and summer.

There were cows on the farm as well as horses and a dairy where often our mistress worked with the three dairy maids. There was always a lot of laughter coming from the dairy and sometimes singing as well. There were two farm men as well as the dairy maids, the older carter Matthew who watched over all us horses though his main duty was to Mermaid and Merlin. A young man called Mooring who did a lot of the other work like cutting the kale and carting it and feeding the pigs. And a boy called Bob, who helped where he was needed. I believe he was Matthew's eldest boy. They all lived on the farm and seemed happy enough – at least I never heard them grumble, though once we heard Matthew talking about something called, 'the general strike'.

'There's no trains at all,' he said. 'And no letters either. I don't know what the world's comin' to. Supposin' we went on strike. Who would feed the animals then?'

'It's all money these days, everyone wants more money. One can't blame them; it's hard enough trying to live on thirty shillings a week, even with a spot of garden,' replied Bill.

'And working all hours as well,' put in Bob.

'But it 'urts everyone in the long run, even the master,' replied Matthew. 'That's the worst of it.'

We were all worried by this conversation. The dairy maids poured away a lot of milk because there were no trains to take it to London. And our master walked about with a worried frown on his face.

My mother said that everything would be all right in the end but we horses sensed that something was wrong. The men had less time for us and there were less oats in our mangers and less singing from the dairy. The general strike ended. No more milk was poured away, but things didn't get any better and after a time one of the dairy maids left.

Our master had little time for us now and one day we heard him saying to Bob, 'It's time you moved on; there's no future in farming any more. No one wants our butter. The world's changing, Bob. I can't afford to give you a rise, and I'm sorry for it because you're a good lad, I've never had a better. But the way things are going, I don't know how we'll be next year.'

Soon after that Bob left. We missed him, especially Sinbad who had been a great friend of his. Our master took off his coat and helped Matthew and Bill himself, which was something he had never done before. He didn't have time to hunt any more, which saddened my mother, who loved hunting more than anything else.

I was four now and black all over except for a splash of white on my left fetlock. My master called me Blackbird. I was used to having my feet rasped, and quiet to groom and handle. No one had ever spoken in anger to me, so that when my master and mistress came to the field gate, I was the first to greet them.

'It's time you were working,' said my master to me one day, stroking my neck. 'When the hay is in, we'll make a start. You should make someone a fine young hunter.' He looked much older and I rubbed my head

12

against his sleeve trying to tell him that I would always do my best.

'Don't do too much, George,' pleaded our mistress, slipping her arm through his. 'Let old Matthew break him in. You know Dr. Simmonds said that you were to rest.'

'Rest!' cried our master. 'When everything is going to rack and ruin. When the bills pile up on my desk and no one wants our butter because New Zealand's butter's cheaper. No, my dear, I can't rest till things are straight.'

'Straight!' she cried. 'They will never be straight till we sell up and go.'

'And that I will never do,' replied our master quietly. 'I was born here. The soil is like a mother to me. And where would we go? I have always been a farmer as my father was before me. I know nothing else, so let's talk no more of going.'

They walked away arm in arm, while my mother shook her head sadly.

'There are bad days ahead for all of us,' she said. 'You are young and strong, Blackbird. Always do your best whatever happens.'

Two weeks later we heard that our master was dead. Gloom hung over the farm, affecting all of us. People think animals don't understand much. But we knew that things were bad. There was no more laughter, everyone looked worried. Matthew feared for his home. His children walked about with their heads down, silently weeping. Bill Mooring stopped tending his garden and was late to work in the mornings. A notice was put outside the farm saying, FOR SALE.

The funeral day was saddest of all. Black horses with plumes on their bridles pulled the hearse and my mother was led behind by Matthew, her saddle empty. All the mourners were in black, our mistress with a veil hiding her face, the children weeping bitterly.

We horses watched the cortège over the field gate, as it wound its sad way to the church less than a mile away.

'We won't be wanted any more,' Merlin said, shaking his wise grey head. 'We will all be sold. And who wants a farm horse these days?'

'I worked in a town once,' said Rosie. 'It was a terrible place. Our stables were high up, with gas lighting. I couldn't bear to go back.'

'I shall be all right,' said Sinbad. 'Children always want piebald ponies. I shall be found a kind home. The children will see to it. Why, our mistress says I'm better than a nanny.'

Mermaid said nothing. She was the oldest of us all and not worth much any more.

Later my mother came back. We all pleaded for news, but first she washed her mouth out at the trough; then she rolled twice, once for each side of her. After that she shook herself and said, 'This is a bad day for all of us. If a good master comes, we will be all right. If not, we will each go our separate ways and most likely never see each other again.'

'But I don't work on the farm. I am separate. I belong to the mistress and the children,' said Sinbad. 'I won't be sold with the farm. They'll find me a good

14

home somewhere.' And he cantered round the field, while the rest of us put our heads down and grazed, each afraid of what the future might hold for us.

CHAPTER TWO

I start a new life

It was not long before we had a new master. He was a young man with hard blue eyes and a moustache waxed at both ends. He had bought the farm cheaply and intended making a profit out of it. He walked round the farm with Matthew, poking the buildings with a stick, laughing at the way things had been run in the past.

'That horse plough can go for a start,' he said. 'I'm not having horses here. The farm is going to be run by machinery. And the hedges will have to go too,' he continued. 'They use up valuable space. If we are to beat the colonies, we can only do it by farming like them.'

Merlin and Mermaid hung their heads in despair. Rosie said, 'That's that then.'

'A lot of trees will have to go too, and the dairy will be modernised. There will be no more dairy maids,' continued our new master.

Matthew touched his cap respectfully. 'And me too, sir? Is my job to be done by machinery?' he asked.

'Yes. We don't need a carter, and you're too old to learn new ways. I shall need your cottage for a younger man. I will give you a week to clear out.'

'But where shall I go?' replied poor Matthew. 'No one is taking on farm hands these days and I'm knocking sixty, sir. I was born in the cottage as my father was before me.'

'That has nothing to do with me,' replied the young

man harshly. 'The cottage is mine now and I can do what I like with it. You can apply to sweep the roads. The council are paying a fair bit these days.'

'But where can I live? And what about my Missus?' asked Matthew.

'That's your business. Now show me the horses. What you do with your life is your own affair. I'm here to make money, and make it I will.'

We stood together in a corner of the field. Matthew called us but we didn't go to him as we usually did. Our new master looked us over as though we were bits of machinery. He did not speak to any of us. We knew he was deciding how much he might get for each one of us. My mother looked quite frightened. She had been treated kindly all her life and talked to as an equal by our poor late master. She had expected to live on the farm until her end came.

At last, our new master spoke. 'The young horse might fetch a bit,' he said staring at me. 'But the others aren't worth much. They can go to the sale at Stansbury next week. I shall be ploughing the field; I'm trying the modern way, one crop one year, one the next. That way you get more out of the land.'

'The master would have wanted them to have good homes. He thought the world of them,' said Matthew.

'And that was his undoing,' snapped back the young man. 'There's no place for sentimentality in modern farming.'

'Shall I be taking them then?' asked Matthew. 'I understand them, sir. I can put in a good word for them; they'll fetch more that way, sir.'

'No. You will be gone by then. I want you out in a week. And I mean a week,' said our new master.

The next day our mistress and the children came to say goodbye. The children cried into Sinbad's mane. Our mistress stroked my mother's nose. 'I'm sorry. He wouldn't have wanted it this way,' she said.

My mother rubbed her nose against her shoulder as she had done to me when I was a foal and needed comforting. The children cried louder than ever. Then they all went away, their arms round each other, and everything was suddenly quiet and I wondered how our field would look with the grass ploughed under and the trees gone.

A few days later a young man, wearing a cap on the back of his head, started moving furniture into Matthew's cottage sighing and grumbling meanwhile.

'Ain't there no water closet?' he asked Matthew. 'And where's the cooking range? How do you manage with the one fireplace?'

'We cooked with a pot hung over it, and reared six children as well,' replied Matthew.

'There's no running water either.'

'There's the well at the bottom of the garden and a good sty for a pig and a couple of old apple trees,' Matthew answered.

When Matthew and his family had gone, we felt as though we had no friend left. No one came to visit us in the evenings to see if we were well. Our water grew low in the trough and we were all bad tempered with worry. Merlin and Mermaid bullied poor Rosie unmercifully and my mother called Sinbad 'an impudent young fool'.

The old farmhouse was empty now and only the young man and a girl milked the cows. Then the day came when we all stood together for the last time under the elm trees. The next morning some rough looking men came, put halters on our heads and led us away from the farm for ever.

It was five miles to Stansbury and we took an hour and a half to reach it. I had never been so far before and I was scared of everything I saw. A man called Jim pulled me along and a man called Fred whipped me from behind while my mother kept whinnying to me in a distracted fashion saying:

'Do your best. Don't be frightened. Follow me.'

But I had never seen a car close up before, nor a bicycle. I could not understand how they moved without legs or heads. People shaking mats out of windows scared me and so did yapping dogs and children playing in the street.

By the time I reached the sale, I was soaked in sweat, with whip marks all over my quarters. There were a great many men shouting, some carrying whips and horses everywhere in all shapes and sizes. There were stalls laden with fruits, and cars going backwards as well as forwards.

It was too much for me. I stopped and stood trembling with fear, my legs braced under me. Jim jerked at my rope. Fred whipped me from behind.

My mother called, 'Don't be afraid. They won't hurt you.' But I was in such a state now that nothing seemed to make sense any more.

If someone had spoken to me kindly then I think I might have calmed down, but all I received was blows from behind and jerks from my halter in front and a flood of bad words. So I stood up on my hind legs and then plunged forward in a wild leap scattering the bystanders. Jim held on, shouting, 'Fetch a bridle.'

A man seized one ear, another my nose. A bit was forced between my teeth, while more men put a rope round my quarters. Then Fred whipped me again and Jim held on to my head while the bit cut my mouth cruelly. All my friends had gone on by this time. The crowd had cleared a space. I was shaking in every limb. I started to spin round and round fighting against the pain of the bit. I reared again, plunged and then came down in a heap on the cobbles. A man in gaiters leapt on my head. I could feel my heart thumping against my ribs and my breath coming in gasps.

'Hold him there for a bit. Let him calm down,' said someone. The bridle had blinkers on it. My mouth was bleeding.

After a time I was allowed to stand again. I was still trembling and my sweat dripped on to the street. A quiet man came and took the reins from Jim. He patted my neck and spoke kindly. 'You shouldn't whip a young horse like that,' he said. 'All he needs is a little kindness.'

He reminded me of our late master though he was a younger man. He had the same quiet strong way with him. I saw my mother tied to a railing in the centre of the square, and still shaking with fright, I was tied up alongside her.

She looked at me sadly, 'If our master could see you now, his heart would be broken,' she said.

I stood tensely, straining against the rope that held me. I shook all over. Men walked up and down looking at us. They forced my mother's mouth open and picked up her hoofs. She was very patient, though I could see how their rough treatment pained her.

No one touched me; one look at my wild eye sent them on to a quieter animal. I think if they had touched my mouth I would have gone mad.

The sale had started now. There was a great deal of noise. A man sat high up holding a hammer while horses were trotted up and down. He shouted all the time and when a horse was sold he banged his

22

hammer on a table. Merlin and Mermaid were separated; their wise heads were furrowed with anxiety. Poor Sinbad stood with his head low, let down by his mistress and the children. Rosie knew about sales; her shoulders were dark with sweat.

Merlin and Mermaid were sold. They neighed piteously to each other as they were led away to await their new owners.

My mother said, 'Always do your best, my son. Man is cleverer than we are; he will always win.' Her turn was next. She went calmly, her head high, her beautiful eyes shining. She trotted steadily over the rough cobbles while the man with the hammer shouted, 'Who wants this twelve year old mare, quiet to ride and with hounds? How much am I bid? Come on, ladies and gentlemen. Fifty pounds, who will bid fifty pounds?'

Men pushed forward to feel her legs, to open her mouth once again with rough fingers. Someone whipped her from behind. She trotted faster over the cobbles, her neck wet with sweat.

I strained against the rope which held me. I neighed: 'Don't go. Don't leave me.'

They wrenched her round on the cobbles and I heard her hoofs slipping. A boy hit her with a stick. Someone said. 'Forty.'

'I'm bid forty,' shouted the auctioneer as though it was a victory.

She was sold for forty-five guineas and led away. Now it was my turn. A man untied me, jerking at my bridle. I trotted over the cobbles, my unshod hoofs making no noise. I couldn't see the crowds on each

23

side because of the blinkers, but when a man touched my quarters I lashed out catching him on the side and I reared when a large-fisted farmer touched my mouth.

The auctioneer shouted, 'Who wants this high spirited young horse? Only four, and what a looker. By a great stallion, out of the mare you've just seen. A certain winner in the right hands. Come along, ladies and gentlemen, how much am I bid?'

I stood with my legs braced trembling with fear. In the distance I heard my mother calling to me.

Then a man in breeches and boots said, 'Well I'll risk him. No horse has beaten me yet.' And people laughed and a man said:

'That's right, have a go, Sid. You can only break your neck once.' A farmer bid twenty. Sid bid twenty-

24

five. I was dragged across the cobbles again. The farmer bid thirty. Sid bid thirty-five. I heard the hammer fall. I was dragged away and tied up with the other horses which had been sold. Mermaid and Merlin were together again. I longed for a drink, but though there was a trough in the square no one watered us.

After a time, Rosie was led away by a bent old farmer.

The town square reeked of beer and sweat and horse dung. A small boy led my mother away. He spoke kindly to her, stroking her neck. I never saw her again.

I stood in the square for a long time. Horses were taken away in ones and twos. The sale ended. Evening came and I still stood tied to the railing longing for a drink.

At last my new master came out of a pub yard leading a chestnut cob. He pushed her between the shafts of a cart. He was unsteady on his feet and it took him some time to buckle the harness.

He tied me to the back of the cart while the cob snapped, 'And don't hang back young fellow. I've got enough to do without pulling you home.'

I felt too exhausted and bewildered to fight any more. In the pubs men were singing. Sid whipped up the cob. My head was sore from pulling against the railings. I could not see much because of the blinkers. I just followed the cart. I don't know how far we went but my unshod hoofs were sore and split when at last we turned into a yard and stopped.

A small man came out of a building with a lantern

in his hand. 'So you're back, Gov,' he said.

'Yes and ready for me dinner,' retorted my new master. 'And I've bought myself a black rogue with the devil in him, for you to pit your wits against, Joe. Put him in the end stall and give him nothing but straw to eat and just one bucket of water. We'll have to starve him before we break him.'

There were rows of stalls inside a long stable. The little man led me to one at the end. He spoke kindly to me and fetched me water and filled the hay rack with oat straw. He looked at my hoofs and sighed. He looked at my teeth with gentle hands and sighed. 'And only a four year old too,' he said.

Then he went away carrying his lantern. The straw tasted rough in my sore mouth. I drank the bucketful of water and was still thirsty. I remembered the field where I had grown up. I thought of Matthew turned out of his cottage with nowhere to go, and the world seemed a rough cruel place.

CHAPTER THREE

I'm broken in

My new master was a horse dealer. He had fought in the Great War and had been wounded in the head. Part of his skull had been replaced by a tin plate and he drank to kill the pain from it. Joe had fought in the war too. He had a scar from his right eye to his left ear and three fingers missing on one hand where they had been blown off by a shell.

They were not bad men, but they had suffered. They had watched men stay at home and make money, while they fought in the trenches. Now they had their own code of honesty which included making money out of us horses by fair means or foul.

My education began the day after I arrived at my new home, which was called Little Heath Stables on account of the rough heath at the back.

In the morning I was given only half a bucket of water and straw again in my rack and not much of that either. I had hardly slept all night and felt weak and listless. There were always nearly twenty horses in the yard and only the two men to look after them;

so only the ones about to be sold were groomed regularly; the rest of us stood in our stalls for hours at a time bored and ill tempered, dreaming of the fields where we had grown up. I stood next to a handsome dark brown gelding called Solomon. He was very well bred and had been a hunter, but had fallen on the road and was now scarred on both knees. Sid was doing what he called, 'doctoring them up', in the hope of making a profit.

My education began with the dumb jockey. It was a strange contraption made of wood and leather straps which Joe strapped on to my back while Sid held my head. Then a bit was forced between my teeth and reins attached from it to the dumb jockey. And so I was left, my head too high for comfort, my nose tucked in towards my chest. I could move little in any direction. I tried pulling, but it hurt my mouth. I tried lowering my head, but that was impossible. In the end I put my hind legs under me to ease the pain and stayed in a sort of sitting position until I could bear it no longer. Next I put my hind legs out behind me and hollowed my loins. Soon my neck muscles suffered from cramp and my hind legs ached unbearably.

I thought, if only we horses could weep like humans, people might know how we suffer. But hours passed and no one came to relieve my agony. Solomon was taken out for exercise and brought back. He looked at me sadly over the partition of his stall.

'They call it mouthing,' he said. 'I wish someone would mouth them.'

My mouth dripped blood on to my scant bedding.

28

Joe was working overtime preparing a rangy bay for a prospective buyer, so it was Sid who came at last to loosen the reins and let me stretch my aching neck. He took the dumb jockey away and fetched me hay and clean water. The bay horse had been sold for a good price and he was cheerful. He called Joe to me.

'He can have hay from now on, but no oats, and give him a brush over when you have time.'

They were not cruel men. Joe worked harder than any of us. He was in the stable by six in the morning and often still there at nine at night. And our master when he was well, was kind enough in his way, but when his head began to ache, he turned to the bottle.

The dumb jockey was the fashionable way to break in a horse in those days and it suited the dealers well enough because it was quick. It broke our spirits and the quicker this was done, the quicker they could sell us and make a profit.

So the next day the contraption was strapped to my back again and, though I longed to fight, I remembered my mother's words, and stood still until my head was strapped into the desired position again. I can't tell you the agony I suffered that day, for my muscles still ached from the day before. I had constant attacks of cramp, my tongue felt swollen in my mouth and my hind legs seemed to have no strength left in them.

For the next three days I wore that dumb jockey for hours every day until gradually the pain became less as I grew accustomed to standing for hours in the unnatural position it demanded.

On the fourth day, Joe attached a long rein to my bridle and led me outside to a small paddock behind the stables. He carried a whip and soon I was trotting round and round him in a circle. It was lovely to smell fresh air again after my dingy stall, but I did wish that I could stretch my neck. However Joe was well pleased. 'He's quick to learn and willing and all the fight's knocked out of him,' he told our master.

Two days later I was shod. Joe talked to me all the time while the shoes were nailed on and the farrier was a quiet, gentle man who took the trouble to make friends with me from the beginning.

After that I was lunged with a saddle on my back and how good it was to be able to stretch my neck. Then my master held my head, while Joe gently slipped on to my back. I was led up and down the paddock and though I felt tense and my joints and muscles still ached from the effect of the dumb jockey, I didn't buck. And so I was broken in. Most of my spirit was gone by this time and my ribs showed through my dirty coat; but there was no fight left in me. I knew now that humans are stronger than us poor horses and however strange their commands we must obey them.

Joe had been a rough rider for the army and he had a firm seat and good hands. He took me for rides when he had time and I soon grew accustomed to the few cars and bicycles which we met, and learned to go how he wished. I looked everywhere for my mother and friends on these rides, but I never saw them. Sometimes I wondered whether they would recognise me if we did meet because I was so much thinner now.

Some weeks later, Sid and Joe started to break me to harness. First of all I pulled a heavy log about the paddock, then I was put in a braking cart and after that in a carriage with another horse of my own size called Tom. He was old and bad-tempered and if I went too fast, he bit me, and if I dawdled he would kick. At first I was very frightened of the sound of the wheels running behind me, but after a few weeks I ceased to notice them and Sid seemed well pleased.

'We can call him quiet in harness now, not that there's much call for harness horses these days,' he said. 'But sometimes it just tips the balance. Now all he needs is some jumping lessons, then he'll be ready for sale and worth a good price too, I should say.'

A few days later, Joe started popping me over logs in the near-by woods and my food was increased. A brush fence and gate were put up in the paddock and soon I was jumping these with ease.

I was now four and a half, and sixteen hands high. Joe began to groom me more and I wore a checked rug in the day and a warmer one at night. My time at the dealer's yard was coming to an end as I was now considered a schooled horse. I could walk and trot on either rein with my nose tucked in. I never pulled against the reins because I knew that a dumb jockey would never give, so I was considered to have a 'good mouth'! I would stand quietly to be mounted and while my rider opened a gate. I could jump fences of three foot six from a trot or canter. I went equally well in a double bridle or snaffle. I would go in harness. I was fast, but no one knew how fast, because, since wearing the dumb jockey, I was afraid to extend myself. I tired easily because carrying my head so near my chest was not natural to me, but to most people who wanted a well-schooled horse, I appeared to be one.

'You wouldn't recognise him as the horse we bought at Stansbury sale,' said Sid one evening, watching Joe rug me up. 'We'll ask one hundred and fifty guineas for him and if we get it, there's a fiver for you, Joe, that's a promise. I'll advertise him this week.'

CHAPTER FOUR

I'm sold again

Two days later an elderly lady came to see Solomon. She had high cheek bones and a voice which expected to be obeyed. She wore breeches with long socks and men's shoes and a khaki shirt. Solomon had been well groomed, his mane was plaited and Joe had covered the scars on his knees with boot polish.

The lady knew how to handle a horse for she went straight to Solomon's head with a lump of sugar in her hand.

'You've known better days, I can see,' she said.

She bent down to look at his knees and then looked at Sid and said, 'You may as well take the boot polish off. I'm not a fool.'

Joe rubbed the polish off with a cloth while Sid hurried off to fetch a side saddle, muttering, 'I can see that, Madam.'

'And I don't need that,' she replied when he returned. 'I ride astride, and I'll have a snaffle bridle please.'

She rode Solomon in the paddock at the back of the stables and afterwards he said that she had the best hands he had ever known.

'And now my man, we'll talk about money,' she said, dismounting. 'I'm not paying what you ask for a start. He's a horse of quality but his legs are ruined, as you no doubt know.' They went away to discuss a price and the next day she brought a man over to ride Solomon to her house. He was a quiet gentle groom, who slipped a snaffle bit into Solomon's mouth with great care and then put a light-weight saddle on to his back as though he was made of china.

'You've fallen into good hands, Solomon old fellow,' he said pulling up the girths. 'No one's going to work you to death. The Countess only hacks around the estate and there's the old pony in the orchard for company. You'll last another twenty years with us.'

I neighed goodbye and he answered with a quick nod of his head. I had never met a finer horse than Solomon. I knew I would miss him but I hoped that at last he had found the happiness he deserved.

The next day a cream mare was moved into Solomon's stall. She was a vain, proud pony with a long flowing flaxen mane.

'What a nasty stall,' she said, looking round with dislike. 'And how it smells! I come from fine stables where I always had my own loosebox. I'm not used to being tied up.'

'You will have to get used to it then,' I replied.

'That I never will. I shall keep turning round until

the head stall rubs me raw; and then I shall dig up the floor and kick the grooms,' she replied with a toss of her head.

'There's only Joe. He won't have time to bother with you,' I answered.

'I'm a weaver. I shall weave then.'

'What do you weave?'

'I keep swaying, moving my weight from one hoof to another. It's a dreadful habit,' she said, starting to do it. 'In my last home I was never exercised; sometimes I stood in my box for days on end, though my mistress visited me every day and gave me sugar and my mane was groomed until it was like spun silk, and my hoofs oiled till they gleamed like polished tortoiseshell. Oh, my mistress loved me all right. She called me her Fairy Queen, but how bored I was! I thought I would go mad with nothing to do day after day. I dreamed of beautiful stallions, of racing the wind. My sides were soon as fat and round as butter. And when at last I was taken out I couldn't trot without puffing. But my mistress thought this beautiful too. "Look how she blows, just like a little train!" she would cry, clapping her plump hands with glee. She didn't mind my weaving either. "It's like a circus trick," she said and she would throw her arms round my neck crying, "Oh Fairy Queen, you are so adorable." '

'She wanted you to be as fat and silly as she was herself,' I said. 'There are many humans like that; we are supposed to resemble them, though we may be quite different. But what about the grooms?' I asked. 'Had they no sense either?'

35

'They followed their orders, though I heard John, the stud groom, saying once that it was a shame to keep me so, and that I would look well in a phaeton or a circus – a circus I ask you? And then one day my feet started to hurt. They felt as though they were swelling and swelling; only hoofs can't swell, can they? The pain was terrible and there was no way of relieving it At last I sank down on the straw and lay there groaning. John found me and then what a hubbub there was! The vet was fetched. I was led outside and stood in a pond and fed branmashes. And I was made to walk though my hoofs felt on fire. How painful that was! And look at my hoofs; they are no longer beautiful; they curl up at the end and everyone can tell that I've had laminitus, and no one wants me now; not even my mistress, though it was her fault. Oh the injustice of it! And how often I longed to gallop, to pull a phaeton and show how fast my little hoofs could trot; but no, my mistress wanted me to be as idle as herself. And now I'm a weaver and my hoofs are spoilt, and I've never done anything; never had any fun.'

I didn't know what to say. Fairy Queen started to dig up her bed. She had been given nothing but musty hay in her rack, which she refused to touch. Soon she was standing on bricks. Then Sid came in.

'What a fool you are, Queenie,' he said. 'Come outside and get some exercise. We can't have you digging up the stable.' She looked pleased and rubbed her nose on his sleeve, and I thought that although Sid was a rough man, at least he understood us.

The next day I was groomed and plaited early and

given an extra ration of oats. 'You behave yourself and you'll find yourself with a good home,' Joe said.

'So you're going,' whispered Fairy Queen from the next stall, 'just when I was beginning to like you. I shall have some cross old horse put next to me for certain. Some crusty old thing which never answers and I shall be more bored than ever.'

'You will be sold soon yourself,' I said. 'You are so pretty, no one will resist you.'

'Not with my weaving and my hoofs. Look at them,' she cried. 'Just look.'

Shortly afterwards Joe came for me. He undid my rope and led me outside to where a young man was waiting, dressed in breeches and boots and a checked jacket with cap to match. He had a small trimmed moustache and carried a cane.

'You'll never find a better horse than this,' said Sid slapping my neck. 'He's not five yet, but he never puts a foot wrong. And as for jumping, well I've never seen one which will beat him.'

The young man was called Richard Bastable. He ran hard, cool hands down my legs. He opened my mouth and checked my age. He stood behind looking at my hocks.

'Trot him up and back. I want to see how he moves,' he said.

Fairy Queen heard my hoofs on the gravel and neighed.

'Yes, he moves well enough,' said Richard Bastable. 'He's for a young lady, so he must have good paces. Now perhaps your man will show me how he jumps.'

Joe threw a saddle on my back; then he put on the twisted snaffle he rode me in normally and mounting, rode me to the paddock. He walked and trotted me to loosen up my muscles; then cantered me in circles while Sid straightened the brush fence and put up the gate. I had stood in the stable for two days with hardly any exercise and was eager to jump; so that when Joe turned me towards the gate, I snatched at the bit and fairly flew.

'What did I say? Jumps like a stag!' exclaimed Sid, rubbing his hands together.

'I do a spot of jumping myself,' said Richard Bastable, sounding pleased.

I jumped the brush again, then they put the gate up to four feet six and I took it easily while Joe stayed as though glued to my back.

Then Richard Bastable mounted. Every rider has his own particular style; Joe gripped tight with his knees, his hands went with you, but if need be, they were like a vice. Richard Bastable rode with longer stirrups, his weight further back in the saddle, his reins longer. At first I missed Joe's firmer grip. I felt like bucking; instead I shied at a bit of paper and pranced a little.

'He hasn't been out for two days,' called Sid anxiously from the gate.

I was determined to do my best. I cantered on either leg, keeping my nose bent inwards, and jumped the fences easily, without fuss.

'I like him,' said Richard Bastable, sliding to the ground. 'I'll pay you what you're asking if he passes the vet.'

'Passes the vet? Of course he will. I'll warrant him sound myself,' exclaimed Sid.

They went inside for a drink, while Joe led me back to my stall. 'I expect you're sold,' said the Fairy Queen. 'I hope it's to a nice home, but I shall miss you terribly.'

Her entire bed was now at the back of her stall, and she had rubbed herself raw fighting against the headstall. Joe hit her from behind. 'Get up, you fool,' he shouted. 'You'll end up pulling a baker's van. It's work you want and plenty of it.'

He rubbed vaseline into her sores, grumbling all the time; then he turned her loose in the paddock. I stood wondering about my new home. I had grown used to Sid's yard. I knew the routine and what Joe wanted. But a loosebox would be nicer than a stall and I dearly wanted to roll again, to lie stretched out in the sun, to sleep under the stars. One way and another I was ready for a move.

CHAPTER FIVE

A new home

Richard Bastable rode me to my new home. It was fifteen miles by roads and lanes. The countryside was pleasant all the way; once we were clear of the heath there were lush meadows on each side full of cows, and little farmhouses nestling in the valleys.

My new master lived in a pretty white house with a cedar tree on the lawn. He was still an unmarried man, but had a housekeeper and Bowles, a cheerful ginger-haired man of around forty who looked after both his motor-car and his horses. There were three of us, myself, a grey hunter, and a brown cob which had pulled my master's dog cart before he had bought a car.

Our stables were modern with four loose boxes which looked towards the house, and when I arrived Richard Bastable took my tack off himself and fetched me hay and water. I was greatly surprised by this, having expected a groom to be waiting for me. He then patted my neck for a long time, saying, 'May will be here tomorrow and what a surprise you'll be.

She's twenty-one tomorrow, quite an age for a young gal and by jove, she's a pretty gal. You'll love her. Everyone does.' Then he went away whistling and the horse in the next box looked over his door and said,

'Who are you? What's your name?'

'I don't know. I'm usually known as the black un,' I answered.

'And that's no name at all,' he replied. 'But they'll soon give you one, at least May will. I'm Warrior. You've come to a good place here. You'll have every attention. Mr. Bastable does a lot himself, though he's a proper young gentleman and Miss May, she's a sweet young lady.'

'I'll do my best,' I answered.

'And that will be good enough for them,' he said.

The next morning a young lady came into the yard. She wore breeches and boots and a riding jacket. She came straight to my box. 'And who are you?' she asked.

'Your birthday present,' cried Richard Bastable bobbing out from behind a tree and hugging her. 'Later we'll drink your health in champagne, but now I want to see how you like him. He hasn't a name. You must choose one for him. He's only five, but he has a mouth like velvet and he jumps like a stag.'

'I shall call him Black Velvet then,' she replied, making friends with me, patting my neck, finding me an apple from under the trees, while Warrior leaned jealously over his door blowing through his nose and stamping his hoofs impatiently.

'Can I try him now?' May asked.

'I don't see why not. He's had a good night's rest.'

Bowles was busy with the car, so they tacked me up together, laughing and kissing one another, so that a happier pair it was impossible to imagine.

'I'll come out with you on old Warrior,' said Richard Bastable. 'He's as jealous as a cat.'

May had light hands and a firm seat. 'He's behind the bit,' she said after a time. 'He must have been broken in with a dumb jockey, poor darling, and now he's afraid to extend himself at all. But his paces are lovely. I shall reschool him. I shall follow Santini's advice and Caprilli's and of course Paul Rodianko's and in a month you won't recognise him.'

'I'm sure I won't,' laughed Richard. 'But why you want to follow the advice of a bunch of foreigners, I can't imagine. But he's yours so do as you like with him.'

Richard Bastable's house was called The Grange. I was happy there. We were well fed and well looked after and best of all whenever the weather was nice we were turned out into one of the paddocks. Miss May's schooling was hard work but pleasant. Slowly she undid all the harm the dumb jockey had done. She made me go forward, driving me on with her legs, she taught me to do shoulder in and shoulder out and how to curve my spine. She taught me to rein back and circle with my neck and back flexed; after two weeks she pronounced me ready to jump and what a revelation that was! I wore only the plainest snaffle and, as we jumped, May leaned forward, her hands going with me so that I could extend myself freely. I found I could jump far more easily in this way, my movements became smoother and more flowing, and though Richard would never admit it was a better way of jumping, I knew it was.

Winter came, and on a lovely frosty afternoon May Chantry and Richard Bastable were married in the grey Saxon church in the village.

We horses were not needed, but we could hear the church bells ringing joyously and everyone seemed happy that day. Bowles whistled and chatted cheerfully to the jobbing gardener who came three days a week. The housekeeper, Mrs. Roberts, announced that there wasn't a better matched pair on earth. 'And I shall pray to God every night that they shall be happy,' she said. 'And have sweet children and everything they want.'

After the wedding they left in Richard's yellow car and we three horses had a holiday. We had not been clipped yet so were turned out every fine day in the paddocks and brought in each night. We liked each other; Warrior was patient and Brandy the cob good natured, so that one way and another we got along very well together. Warrior had gone to the Great War as a four year old and was one of the few in his regiment to come back. Brandy had been a farmer's cob. Neither had been ill-used or beaten and because of that they were happy and contented with no vice in them.

We were clipped before our master and mistress returned from their honeymoon and that winter they hunted us regularly, always bringing us home before we were too tired. Bowles would be waiting for us, the electric light shining out from the stables, our loose boxes deeply bedded in deep golden straw. The three of them would settle us for the night together and there were always hot mashes with salt and grated carrot in them. So the winter passed and spring came and I was very fit now and moved easily and well. I had jumped many a five barred gate in the hunting field and my master wanted to ride me in point-to-points, but this my mistress forbade.

'Too many men have been killed racing,' she said. 'And I couldn't bear to lose you, Richard; besides, two races with you would undo all my schooling. No, Richard darling, I intend to show jump him this summer, if you have no objection.'

'None at all, though I don't suppose you'll have much luck. I've yet to see a lady rider beat the gentlemen,' he replied laughing.

'Then I shall be the first,' she replied.

So Bowles was put to building jumps and, while Warrior and Brandy lounged about the paddocks, my mistress schooled me, always riding me forward in the Italian style. I was very careful.

If I hit anything May would scold me and I would feel ashamed and jump better next time. She never lost her temper and when I jumped well she would dismount at once, reward me with sugar, and that would be the end of the lesson. She taught me slowly, never making the jumps too high or too difficult until I was ready for them. One day Richard was watching and he called out, 'By jove, he's doing well. How about the local show next month? There's a novice class and not too many entries, I believe.'

'How high are the jumps?'

'Not more than three foot six, but they might go

45

higher in a jump off,' replied Richard.

'Well, I've jumped him over five foot in the hunting field and four foot six at home, so that should cause Black Velvet no headaches,' said my mistress, patting my neck. 'Let's enter him tonight, and if he jumps well there we can go on to something better before the summer's gone.'

I felt very proud as I returned to my stables. Neither Warrior nor Brandy had ever competed at a show, nor had my mother.

'We must win, Black Velvet,' said my mistress, taking off my bridle. 'We must show everyone that the forward seat is best. People may laugh at me in the hunting field for the way I sit over fences, but they won't laugh any more if they see us winning prizes. Then they may lean forward too and stop trying to hold up their poor horses by brute force, and there will be a lot of happier horses around.'

Warrior shook his head. 'They won't take a blind bit of notice of a lady,' he said to me afterwards. 'Now if it was the master, things might be different.'

I knew he was jealous, so I said nothing more about it, but I made up my mind that I would do my best, come what may.

CHAPTER SIX

A show

Many of the horses I had met hunting were at the show. The master's bay, called Benjamin, was there and a subscriber's flashy chestnut mare called Wildfire. There was the cob, Moonlight, which carried an old lady to hounds, ridden by his groom, and a roan pony of fourteen two ridden by a girl. May had plaited my mane. Bowles had groomed me till my coat shone like black ivory.

Of course, I had never been to a show before, so everything was new to me. But May was calm and kind. She talked to me and let me look around, so that when it was my turn to go into the ring I was quite at home.

I shall never forget that first competition. I felt so proud to be carrying my mistress. She was the only lady competing and I was determined to do my best.

The first jump was a brush fence, the second a gate. May allowed me to gallop on. I heard someone say, 'It's a lady, astride too, well I never.'

'And what a pace she's going,' commented someone else.

Then we were turning towards the wall. It was painted red and grey and I snorted a little with surprise.

'Go on, it's all right,' said May. 'You can do it, Velvet.'

I could feel the strength and determination in her hands through the reins. I increased my pace and then we were over the wall and cantering on towards the stile. This was a narrow fence and like all the other fences had thin slats of wood along the top, and, if you knocked one of these down, you were given half a fault. But I didn't touch anything. An in-and-out followed the stile and then some rails. Another second and we were racing down the centre to the last and largest jump, the triple. May urged me on and then we were over and the crowd was cheering and someone shouted, 'A clear for Black Velvet ridden by Mrs. Bastable herself.'

Richard Bastable met us. 'By jove, that was great,' he cried. 'Well done both of you!'

May slipped to the ground and filled my mouth with sugar.

In the ring the jumps were being put up.

'There's one other clear,' said Richard, 'so you'll have to go round again.'

'The forward seat must win,' said May. 'Leg me up again, Richard.'

The jumps were higher, but it didn't matter. I think I could have jumped anything that day. Benjamin went first with the master of our hounds riding him, but he brought the slats down off the wall and refused the gate.

I was prancing to go in. I knew I could do it and I did. I came out to a great roar from the crowd and then May rode me in again to stand first in the ring.

'That was pretty good for a lady, Mrs. Bastable,' said the judge, lifting his bowler hat.

'That was the forward seat in action, Colonel Rivers,' replied May quickly. 'It has nothing to do with being a lady.'

Benjamin snapped at me, 'I can still beat you in the hunting field.'

'We'll see about that next season,' I said, arching my neck proudly.

After that we went to several shows and I was always in the first three.

At one a large man on a half-hackney half-thoroughbred offered three hundred pounds for me.

But May only laughed. 'I wouldn't sell him for all the tea in China,' she said.

'I could make him into one of the best jumpers in England,' replied the man. 'So don't forget, will you? The name is Chambers.'

'I shall forget just as soon as I can,' replied May, 'because you jump with the backward seat and I with the forward. If I sold Black Velvet it would be to a rider who practised the forward seat. Good afternoon, Mr. Chambers.'

A year passed pleasantly, then another and another. They were happy years. We were content, well fed and well ridden. Then a blow fell on us all like a thunderclap out of the sky.

It happened one early morning when May was helping Bowles to groom us. Richard came rushing out of the house with a newspaper in his hand.

He didn't see Bowles but rushed straight to May. 'We are ruined,' he said. 'I've lost everything, I gambled it all and lost!'

'But on what?' she asked only half believing.

'On pepper.'

'On pepper?'

'On shares, on pepper shares!' he cried. 'Oh what does it matter on what? It's gone. All of it.'

May turned pale. She put my rug straight with trembling hands. 'But there's still *my* money,' she said at last.

'It's gone too. I gambled it too.'

'What, all of it?'

'Yes, every penny. Oh I was mad, I see that now. I

thought I was going to make a fortune for both of us. I can't forgive myself.'

May shut my box door. 'Will we have to go, leave, sell up . . . ?' she asked, her voice shaking.

'Yes, everything . . . '

I could see tears trickling down her face. 'How could you? You fool,' she said quietly. 'How could you let us all down?'

We watched them go into the house together, filled with foreboding.

'We will be sold,' Brandy said. 'I shall pull a hay cutter and you will be worked to death.'

'I shall go to the kennels,' said Warrior. 'I'm good for nothing else.'

The house had been mortgaged. The mortgage couldn't be paid. May came to the stables and wept. Men appeared with vans and took the furniture away. Bowles stopped coming. The yellow car was driven away by a strange man in a peaked cap.

Then one morning, May came into the stable and stood weeping with her face buried in my mane. Richard soon followed. He seemed a changed man.

'I will be master in my own house,' he shouted. 'I tell you, Velvet will go to Mr. Chambers whatever you say. We can't refuse three hundred guineas.'

'You gave him to me. He was my birthday present,' wept May.

'That was years ago. Things were different then.'

'Yes, they were,' replied May, with much misery in her voice.

'Well I've sold him anyway,' replied Richard

53

roughly. 'Mr. Chambers is fetching him after lunch and a dealer's coming for the other two. Black Velvet will have a good home. He will become a champion jumper and he loves jumping, and just forget about the forward seat . . . It's not important.'

May fed us the last of the oats. 'I can't bear to see them go,' she said in a broken voice. 'You must load them up, or send them off, which ever it is, Richard. I can take no more. If only you had given me time, I could have found them all good homes.'

'There is no time,' Richard replied. 'I owe everyone money and they must be paid somehow.'

'But why did you have to gamble? We were so comfortable,' she said. 'Why?'

'I don't know myself. It's like a madness,' he said.

So we all went our different ways. A horse box came for me and Mr. Chambers himself led me up the ramp. He was a heavy man with a red face and a loud voice.

'Tell your Missis, he'll be all right with me and that she'll see him jumping at Olympia before I've done with him,' he said.

'I will, I will,' replied Richard Bastable in a distraught voice.

I had never travelled in a horse box before. I found it rough at first, but after a time I learned to keep my balance and travelled comfortably enough.

Mr. Chambers kept a farm with six or seven loose boxes for his show jumpers. The boxes were comfortable though the doors were too low for a horse of my size, and if I was scared suddenly I frequently hit my head on the roof. However there was plenty to eat and good company and I thought at first I would be happy. I liked show jumping and, though Mr. Chambers was much heavier than my late mistress, I was determined to do my best and win him many prizes.

CHAPTER SEVEN

A beating

Sometimes determination and goodwill are not enough. I wanted to win and I did, to begin with. I could jump round novice classes from a walk. But when the jumps were over four foot I needed to stretch myself, to go on a bit. May had taught me to jump like that and I could jump anything given my head. But my new master had other ideas. He liked his horses to jump with precision. He rode at the fences at a slow collected canter and he never let go.

Even when we were in the air we could still feel his heavy hands on our mouths. Without being snobbish, I must say that his other horses were not as well bred as I am. Most of them had carthorse blood and they could stand heavy hands and pain better than I could.

I fought my master and because I fought him, I couldn't attend to the jumps and knocked them. I grew careless and disheartened; all I wanted was room to extend myself, nothing more. But he wouldn't give in to me. He changed my bit for a stronger one which hurt my mouth. I stuck my head in the air to avoid the pain, so he attached a martingale. I fought against the martingale, so he attached another one. I shook my head, so he changed the bit to a curb.

I went on hitting the jumps so he attached hedgehog skins to them to prick my legs. The pricks from the skins made me more frantic, because I wanted a chance to jump in my own fashion and avoid them; so my forelegs were bandaged with tin tacks in the bandages. Sometimes I thought I would go mad. The other horses were friendly enough. 'Go the way he wants. Stop fighting. Humans are stronger than us. Give in,' they said.

I wished I could. I wished I could jump the fences slowly like they did, but I wasn't built that way.

I couldn't jump out of a slow canter. I had not their short springy action which made it possible. Soon I was dreading shows and even more the endless practising beforehand. Mr. Chambers was an obstinate man. He had paid a good price for me and he didn't mean to be done. When the hedgehog skins and tin tacks failed, his groom would rap me as I went over. Bert the groom was not a bad man, he merely did what he was told. He never gave us a kind word nor did he beat us or ill use us in the stable, our boxes were none too clean but they were mucked out once a day and there was no shortage of food or bedding.

I don't think he liked the rapping, I heard him say once, 'It won't do any good with a high spirited horse like Velvet.' But my master didn't listen. He didn't listen to anyone, not to his poor frightened mouse-like wife, the vicar nor anybody else. He was a law unto himself.

So Bert ran with a long stick and as I jumped, he hit my legs trying to make me jump higher.

And soon I was looking at him instead of the jumps so that sometimes I hardly jumped at all.

One day, my master lost his temper completely and beat me viciously. He swore and shouted and said that if I didn't jump he would shoot me, while I stood dripping with sweat and trembling all over, my head strapped down, my bandages full of tin tacks, my legs bleeding. His wife chose to come across the field then with a mug of tea for him, but he knocked it straight out of her hand.

'Wouldn't a little kindness be better?' she asked in a timid voice. 'A little kindness all round?'

Another day a man was riding past on a splendid thoroughbred and stopped to watch. After I had been thoroughly beaten he called from the gate, 'Can I make a suggestion?'

'I don't want any suggestions, I've been riding since I was four. I don't need help from anyone,' shouted back my master.

'I just want to say that no animal can jump with his head strapped down like that,' shouted the stranger. Beating won't help. He can't jump like that, poor devil.'

But my master made no answer, so after a moment the stranger rode on.

At last the show-jumping came to an end and we were clipped for the hunting season. My mane was hogged to save trouble and I was hunted in the same dreadful curb and the two martingales. I did my best, but my master was a heavy man. He leaned back over every jump and thirteen stone on your quarters is no help when you have been hunting all day and there are still high fences to be jumped. No one knew me in this part of the country and I doubt whether they would have recognised me if they had, for my coat was a dull black now which no amount of grooming would alter, my mane was gone, and I did not go well any more, but fought and shook my head unceasingly.

My master was for ever jerking at my mouth and shouting, 'Walk you b . . . horse.' But I could not walk well with my head strapped towards my chest by two martingales.

That winter was the worst I had suffered. I felt years older when spring came with the first shows. Mr. Chambers had been certain that 'a spot of hunting' would put me right, but it hadn't. I was more run down and nervous than ever.

The bandages were put on again with the tin tacks; the hedgehog skins were nailed to the poles. Bert and Mrs. Chambers held wire above the fences which they raised as I went over to catch my legs and make me jump higher, but still the slats fell.

I went to the shows with the other horses. Last season I had won too much to be classed a novice any more, so the jumps were higher now. I fought more. I refused to go into the horse box without a fight, I refused to enter the collecting ring.

One day I felt a soft hand on my neck and heard a voice say, 'Velvet.' I was sweating, waiting to go in, dreading every moment which was to follow.

I turned and saw that it was May. She had changed too, she was thinner, sadder. She stroked my neck and said, 'Do you need two martingales and a curb, Mr. Chambers? Once he had a mouth like velvet.'

My master looked down at her. 'He's mine now, Mrs. Bastable,' he said. 'And I will ride him in what I like.' He dug his spurs into my sides and a moment later we were in the ring. I never saw May again.

I cleared five fences but I could not jump the spread fence that followed. It was four feet high and wider than I had ever jumped before. I came into it far too slowly and stopped. You need speed to jump a spread. I tried again while my master spurred me on, holding me at the same time with his hands, and I knew I couldn't do it. The third time I jumped, but landed in the middle of the poles and my master fell

into them very slowly. The crowd laughed loudly, while my master stood up his face red with fury and I stood waiting trembling in every limb.

He remounted and we jumped the last fence and

left the ring. He took me to the box and called Bert.

'Shut up the ramp when he's in. We're going to give this one a lesson for all time,' he said.

'Do you think it will do any good?' Bert asked, leading me up the ramp.

'Yes, he's still fighting. He's got to be mastered. When he's mastered, he'll jump.'

Bert said no more. They threw up the ramp and climbed back into the box and laid into me with whips. My master calling all the while, 'That will teach you a lesson, you stupid animal. That will teach you to make me a laughing stock.' I reared up and hit my head. I ran backwards but I couldn't escape. When they had had enough they left me still in my tack with my girths still tight. Bert came back after a while with the other horse which had come with us. He was a thick-set cob called Gimlet. 'I told you man is stronger Why do you go on fighting? You'll always get the worst of it. Just do your best,' he said.

'But I can't.' I answered, 'not in a curb with my head strapped in. I wish I could.'

After that dreadful day, things went from bad to worse. I lost my nerve completely. I started to refuse at every show. Bert and my master beat me unmercifully and one day, when I saw my chance, I fought back. I started to kick. I caught Bert on his arm and my master on his back and then suddenly everything was quiet, the shouting stopped, the whips were still. Then I saw that Bert was holding his arm saying, 'It's smashed,' in a surprised voice. And that my master was lying in a corner of the box without moving.

A little later some men came and let down the

ramp and carried away my master. Still later Bert returned with his arm in a sling, and took off my tack. 'I always knew it would end like this,' he said in a subdued voice. ' 'Im and his temper, and all that drink as well.'

A strange man drove the box home. Another man came to help Bert with us horses. The next day I learned that I had broken my master's back and that he would never ride again. We were all to be sold at once, I with my reputation in ruins.

CHAPTER EIGHT

I'm sold again

We were sent to a sale. There was much interest in the other jumpers, but news travelled and no one would look at me for a jumper.

I felt very dejected though Bert stood up for me as best he could, saying, 'He's not a bad horse. It was the master's temper which did it. He's not a vicious animal . . . '

Finally a man with a hook nose and blue veins on his face opened my mouth and said, 'He's quite a young horse though his legs have been banged about.'

'That's jumping,' replied Bert quickly. 'It isn't work that's done it. If you want a cheap horse, he won't fetch much and there's plenty of work still in him.'

The man ran his hands down my legs and looked into my eyes.

'I don't like blacks myself,' he muttered.

Later he bid for me, standing firmly in the crowd with his legs far apart, one thumb in his waistcoat pocket. There was only one other bidder and I was sold to Mr. Smith for the small sum of thirty pounds.

Soon afterwards he mounted a bicycle from which he led me home.

My new owner lived five miles from a town and ran a hiring stable.

His stables were dilapidated; built of packing cases and corrugated iron, they leaned lopsided against a bank. There were no windows and what air there was came through the gaps in the walls. There were horses standing in stalls but none of them raised their heads when I entered; they were all too busy picking up wisps of musty hay from the floor.

My stall was at the end. I was offered water from a trough; then tied to a ring in the wall. There was a pile of musty hay in a corner. I was accustomed to wearing a rug; to moving about a loose box, but at least here there were no tin tacks or hedgehog skins. The whole place smelt damp and dirty. I heard my master shut a door and latch it. All was total darkness now.

An ugly horse showing much white in his eye raised his head and sniffed. 'And who are you?' he asked.

'I'm Black Velvet, a show jumper.'

'You won't show jump here,' he answered.

I felt very miserable. I knew I was going down in the world. There was damp sawdust under my feet and the hay was hard and tasted damp.

'You'll catch lice,' said another voice. 'We all have lice.'

'Don't talk, please don't talk. I'm so tired and to-morrow is Saturday,' said a plaintive voice from the other end of the stable.

'And what happens on Saturday?' I asked.

'You'll soon know,' replied the ugly horse next to me. 'Don't talk any more. We must rest.'

I spent a restless night, racked by hunger and thirst. In the morning I could see the other horses better. There were not many of us, and the others looked a motley crowd. Their ribs stood out, their quarters had deep poverty marks; their poor necks were thin and looked as scraggy as a crow's neck. Most of their hoofs needed shoeing; their eyes were dull and listless.

We were all offered stagnant water from the trough; then more hay was brought and dumped on the floor of our stalls.

The ugly horse next to me said, 'You look fat enough, young fellow. But you won't stay that way long.'

A small pony snickered. 'Here come the potato peelings.'

'I'm Major, that's Silver,' said the ugly horse.

The potato peelings were tipped into our mangers, which smelt rancid, our master shouting all the time, 'Get over will you. Stand up, or I'll teach you a lesson.'

He was very rough with me, jerking at my head muttering, 'And if you so much as lift a hoof, you're for it.'

After that we were brushed with an assortment of worn-out brushes and then a strange collection of saddles were brought in. Most of them needed stuffing. Major had an old piece of blanket put under his and wads of cotton wool stuffed under his girth. He stood resting a foreleg, his old head hanging, deep hollows above his eyes.

Further down a mare called Mouse wore a new saddle which looked as though it had never been cleaned. Her withers were high, her poor back very thin from lack of food. She looked very weak. 'I shan't last much longer. I know I shan't,' she said.

'She used to pull a cab by the seaside,' said Major, without raising his head. 'She has been here some time, about five years she thinks. She was here when I came.'

Silver wore a felt saddle. He must have been a pretty pony once, but now his tail was stained yellow, and his eyes had a dull, hopeless look about them.

'What is this place?' I said to Major.

'A hiring stable they call it. People come here from the town to ride us; it's fashionable you see among the town folk. They don't know anything of course; if they did, they wouldn't come, would they?'

'Yes they would,' replied Silver. 'They wouldn't care. They couldn't ride us if we were well; we would be too lively for them.'

'I will never be lively again,' said Mouse.

'Nor I,' agreed a large grey, white with age. 'I find it hard to trot. I'm always stumbling; one day I shall fall and won't have the strength to get up again.'

'That's old Twilight. He carried a master of hounds when he was young. He's never forgotten it.'

An old hunting saddle was put on my back and then two bits were forced into my mouth, a curb and bridoon. The curb had a port and curb chain.

'That's it then, Jake,' said my new master. 'You

just behave yourself and you'll be all right.'

We were all ready now and presently our riders started to arrive. They wore all sorts of clothes. Some carried hunting whips, others sticks cut from hedges, one man came in boots and spurs and a young lady even rode in shorts.

They came in droves, all day long with hardly a break. We always went the same way – up a lane across three fields, through a wood and back down the lane again. Most of the riders knew nothing, though I was given the best. They didn't consider us and we were forced to canter along the rough lane, and often to gallop through the fields however tired and blown we were.

Twilight was given all the heavy riders. They sat far back in the saddle and many couldn't so much as rise, but hung on by the reins. He looked very tired and dejected and stumbled constantly. Mouse was given the ladies to carry; they were lighter, but they sat anyhow and talked and smoked and kicked her incessantly with unsuitable shoes. As the day wore on, her poor neck seemed to grow thinner and several times she stopped to cough.

I felt very dejected. I wanted to do my best, but carrying one heavy handed rider after another took every ounce of pleasure away. As I have said, I was given the best riders, but they rode me hard. By evening the soles of my hoofs were bruised from the stones in the lane and my back ached.

Work ended with darkness. Our master collected his last few miserable shillings, and led us to our stalls. Our saddles were removed. Our bridles taken away. We stood patiently waiting without moving; too tired to protest at anything. Twilight lay down. Outside there was a dark sky and a rising moon; inside it was humid with an overpowering smell of horse dung.

After a time we were watered and given hay; then the door was shut and the day was over. Though we were hungry, we ate slowly. A rat ran from manger to manger. Mice squeaked around our hoofs.

Presently Mouse lay down. There was no sound from Twilight's box.

'Sunday is worse than Saturday,' said Major. 'My off fore is very painful tonight.'

'I've lost a shoe,' said Silver.

'If it rains they won't come, no one will come,' said Major.

Twilight was dead in the morning; his poor grey head pathetic on the dirty yellow sawdust. Our master said it was old age which killed him, but we knew differently.

'I shall be the next,' Mouse said. 'I keep coughing. I hope it will be soon.'

They tied ropes round Twilight's thin fetlocks and dragged him away. We were very sad.

'You will carry all the heavyweights now,' Major told me. 'He knew Twilight wouldn't last much longer.'

Sunday was worse than Saturday. People kept asking where the old grey was.

'Died in the night,' our master said. 'It was very sad. He must have had a weak heart.'

'Poor old thing, what a shame,' said our riders. 'We

shall miss him. There's' nothing like a white horse.'

Mouse looked very dejected. It was a dry warm day with a cloudless blue sky. The wood was full of flies; the ground in the fields was hard and unyielding to our tired legs.

Men rode me in ancient hunting boots, in shiny black shoes, in trousers, in plus fours. 'He's terrific,' they said. 'Can I have him next week? He's very fast.'

My mouth was sore now and bleeding at the corners. They gave me lumps of sugar and said that I should be called Highwayman.

They came and went, pressing shillings into our master's hand, until at last darkness came like a welcoming blanket to shield us from work.

We lumbered exhausted into our stalls. Twilight's was empty, reminding us that our turn might not be long in coming.

'They could ride bicycles. Why must they ride us?' asked Silver.

'It's fun,' replied Major bitterly.

We were given old cabbage leaves mixed with chaff and a handful of oats. Our master was in a hurry because he wanted to spend some of what we had earned at the pub. He didn't wait for us to drink our fill of water. Ten minutes after the last saddle was taken off, the doors were shut.

Major was resting his off fore again. 'It's Monday tomorrow. We'll have more of a rest.'

Mouse was coughing; after a time she lay down. We were all afraid she would die in the night, but in the morning she was still there.

Soon I had lice like the other horses. They sucked my blood and my skin itched and I felt ill tempered. A little powder would have killed them, but our master either didn't know or didn't care.

Day followed day. I grew thinner. My feet had thrush in them. My eyes smarted from a combination of sawdust and ammonia. I began to tire easily. I was popular with the customers and one day one of my regular riders asked to take me hunting.

'Hounds are meeting just over the hill. I'd like to take my young lady as well. She's never been hunting before,' he said.

I could see our master hesitating. He knew how badly fed we were; no doubt he was wondering whether I could stand up to a day's hunting.

But the young man was persistent. 'My young lady would like Mouse,' he said. 'And we'll pay a pound for each. We won't go fast.'

He took two pound notes from his wallet and held them in one hand.

There was a short silence. 'Make it two pounds ten shillings,' said our master, his eyes shining at the sight of money.

'Fair enough.'

'What time do you want them?'

'The meet is at eleven at The Horse and Groom. So ten o'clock will do. We'll want a drink at the meet,' said the young man, lighting a cigarette.

CHAPTER NINE

The hunt

Next day and the day after Mouse and I were fed oats. We were groomed with extra care and on the third day we were fed early and had our tails bandaged and our hoofs oiled.

Then we were led outside to stand in the yard waiting the arrival of our riders. It was a misty morning with dewy cobwebs still festooning the hedgerows. Poor Mouse stood with drooping head and straggling legs. I felt better for the oats. The air felt fresh and I longed for the cry of hounds.

Presently the young man, who was called Dick, and his girl friend Jane arrived. They both wore bowler hats. Jane wore an ordinary tie, checked coat, breeches and wellington boots. Dick wore a white cravat, a black coat with tails, white breeches, black boots with spurs attached. They were soon mounted and riding away, laughing and talking together. Mouse had not my long stride and found it difficult to keep up. She coughed twice and kept trying to turn back towards the stables. We met a few cars on the road and a great many bicycles with people on their way to the meet.

Quite soon we saw hounds and a collection of horses outside a pub. Our riders pushed us on. Mouse coughed again, while Jane bumped up and down on her back, sometimes rising, sometimes not.

Outside the pub all was merriment. Dick fetched drinks and they sat on our backs laughing, smoking and drinking, calling the hounds 'dogs', and everyone in a pink coat a huntsman. People looked at us curiously. Someone said, 'That mealy mare over there looks poor, doesn't she, nothing but skin and bone?' But Dick and Jane did not hear, or if they did they pretended otherwise. Presently we moved off, Dick and Jane talking all the while and bouncing up and down on our poor backs like balls on a tennis court.

Hounds drew a copse. Dick lit a cigarette. Mouse hung her head. Soon there was a holla from the far side and I, intoxicated as usual by the sound of the horn and the cry of hounds, forgot poor Mouse and galloped wildly across a field in the wake of fifty horses. But Dick yelled over his shoulder, 'Come on, Jane. We're getting left. Use your crop, dammit.'

I reached into my bridle, my sore mouth forgotten, my heart thudding against my side, ready to go until I dropped. Dick pulled me up at the top of a hill and waited. Mouse was coughing again. Dick was angry and red faced.

'We are missing everything,' he yelled. 'Make the blasted mare go,' and he thrashed her himself with his own lash and thong.

76

I could see the hurt in Mouse's eyes as we went on. Her breathing was laboured now. Jane held on to the saddle with both hands. Hounds were checking. Dick stopped me and waited; then we rode on more slowly. 'We've hired a dud. That's obvious,' said Dick angrily. 'She just can't or won't keep up.'

'I have been whipping her,' said Jane. 'When she gets her breath she'll go better.'

Sweat was dripping off Mouse's side, her neck was lathered with it. She looked at me and said nothing. I thought, if we could only speak or weep.

Then hounds found once more and we were off. We checked again in a field with sheep bunched in one corner. Dick lit a cigarette, his hands trembling with rage. Jane was beating Mouse up a hill without mercy. I thought she was going to die; there was agony in her eyes and her nostrils were extended and her breath was coming in sobs. A farmer on a cob was watching. He rode up to Jane yelling, 'Put down that whip. Leave her alone. Do you want a dead horse under you? Get off at once. Loosen the girths.'

Jane dismounted reluctantly. 'I don't know where the girths are,' she said in a plaintive voice.

The farmer dismounted and let the girths out himself. 'You should be ashamed of hunting a horse in that condition,' he said. 'She's nothing but skin and bone and her wind's broken. Now you take her straight home before I have the police or an RSPCA Inspector after you. Where do you come from?'

'Mr. Smith's livery stables. We've hired these two horses. We've paid a good price for a day's hunting and that's what we intend to have,' said Dick.

'And that you won't have,' replied the farmer. 'You take your poor animal home this minute or I'll speak to the master myself.'

'We paid the Secretary,' replied Dick. 'And hunt we will.'

'I'm going home,' replied Jane. 'Before Mouse dies. Just look at her, Dick, and have mercy.'

'And there's a sensible young lady. There's some things beyond and above money; there's some things money won't buy – and one is a clear conscience,' replied the farmer.

And now a lady had joined the farmer. She looked at us with pity. 'Someone should be prosecuted,' she said.

'Don't worry, m'lady,' replied the farmer. 'I shall be seeing Mr. Smith tonight. I shall see this never happens again.'

'We had better go,' Dick said. 'Get up on your wretched horse, Jane.'

'I would rather walk,' she replied, fondling Mouse. 'If only I had known I would never have come. What is a broken wind?'

'It's her lungs. They've been strained,' said the lady.

'Won't she ever get well?'

'No.'

'Poor Mouse.' Jane was crying now. She walked away leading Mouse, with Dick reluctantly following. The hunt had vanished, but the farmer and the lady set off in hot pursuit, while Dick jerked me in the mouth and kicked me with his spurs and Jane walked with one arm over Mouse's neck weeping bitterly and muttering over and over again, 'If only I had known.'

We were earlier than expected and Mr. Smith was not at home.

Dick knocked on the back door of the house and after a while, Mrs. Smith answered. 'Tie them to the wall,' she said. 'They will be all right there.'

'Mouse needs a veterinary surgeon,' called Jane, 'she's ill.'

'He will attend to that. He understands horses. Just leave them. You have paid, haven't you?' she asked.

'Yes, and far too much,' replied Dick, angrily turning on his heel.

They tied us to two rings on the stable wall by our reins; my girths were still too tight. Mouse looked very tired.

Jane wanted to stay and wait, but Dick insisted that if they were quick they could have a drink before the pubs closed. He swung his car with a handle, grumbling all the time about Mr. Smith's dishonesty in sending out two unfit horses.

When they were gone everything was quiet and I could hear Mouse's laboured breathing. She tried to lie down but the reins were tied too tightly to the wall. She coughed and started shivering. A cold wind whipped round the yard and soon I was cold too and very thirsty. Slowly afternoon turned to evening and then at last Mr. Smith returned whistling merrily. He was surprised to see us back, but soon had us inside the muggy stable. Mouse lay down at once with a sigh and was not interested in her hay, or the oats he brought later. None of us felt like talking. I think we were all too worried about Mouse.

Then we heard a great commotion outside and the farmer who had sent us home from hunting, rushed into the stable with Mr. Smith on his heels.

'This place should be pulled down,' he shouted furiously. 'What are you feeding your animals on? Let me see. Come on, show it to me, or by George I'll have you prosecuted.'

Then he saw Mouse and kneeling down beside her he said, 'And how are you, pet? so gently that he might have been speaking to his own child. He stroked her poor thin neck and put his hand against her labouring sides. She raised her head a little and nuzzled him.

He put his head against her side and listened to her

heart. He stood up slowly and stared at Mr. Smith, muttering, 'Poor little mare.'

'She needs a vet,' he said. 'I'll send mine over at once. I think it's too late, and while I'm away I expect these other horses to be properly fed and watered. Try the mare with a mash, a nice warm bran mash with some treacle in it.'

He looked round the stable in disgust, kicking the sawdust with the toe of a hunting boot. He picked up a wisp of hay and smelt it. Then he patted us each in turn, muttering 'Poor horses, poor old devils,' and left.

Later a man came in a car. Mr. Smith took him straight to Mouse. We had all been well fed by now and the sweat had been brushed from my coat. They were a long time with Mouse. They wanted to take her outside, but she wouldn't move. We heard Mr. Smith say, 'She's only twelve,' and the other man replied, 'More's the pity.' And there was a bang which made us all jump in our stalls and Major said quietly, 'She's gone.'

After that, we were given better hay and more of it and at least one feed of oats and chaff a day. But the work was harder without Twilight and Mouse and I could feel my strength going. My legs had windgalls and were often stiff in the mornings from lying on damp sawdust. Then in March Mr. Smith bought a new horse, a big chestnut named Starlight. He was a handsome horse with badly scarred knees. He soon became a great favourite with all the better riders and I found myself carrying most of the beginners. We now had our diet supplemented with cut grass and sometimes a boy would help in the stables at the weekends. I was so quiet now that my double bridle was changed for a snaffle which was more comfortable.

The blacksmith painted the inside of my hoofs with some tar which cured my thrush and sometimes on Mondays we were turned out in a small paddock behind the stables. Here we would tell each other our life stories while we stood head to tail swishing at the flies.

CHAPTER TEN

Another war

I won't dwell on the next few years. Gradually life grew worse again. Another Christmas came and passed. Major's leg became worse until even our customers complained that he was lame. So one beautiful day he was taken out and shot. We all missed him a great deal.

Then Silver was hit by a car and after that shied a good deal and was considered unsafe. He was sent to a sale and we never saw him again. Starlight developed ring bone and complained constantly about the pain in his hoof. A new horse was bought who reared and broke a young man's arm. He was sold for dogs' meat, I believe. A bay mare came, a kind hard-working animal who because of her willingness did a great deal of work. Another year passed. My eyes were very bad by this time and my coat had come out in patches.

I stumbled a good deal and sometimes I wished I could just lie down and die as Twilight had. More children came to ride us and at least they were light and anxious to please. A skewbald pony was bought for them and called Clown. He talked a great deal about things I had never heard of.

'My last owner was a member of the Pony Club,' he said. 'It's a club formed to make people understand us better, to give us a better life. He would take me to rallies and gymkhanas.' But after a time Clown's enthusiasm faded and he became like the rest of us, depressed and dejected. I was known as Old Jake now; I was fifteen years old with a hollow back and deep hollows above my eyes.

I still tried to do my best, but the weekends seemed to grow harder and our food less plentiful. Our master had aged too. He moved more slowly and his face grew increasingly red. One day his wife was taken away to hospital on a stretcher and after that he was more bad tempered and drank more.

Tractors ploughed the fields now and it was rare to see a horse pulling a plough as Mermaid and Merlin had long ago. I often thought about the past but mostly about May and how happy I had been at The Grange.

Then one day our master came into our stable very drunk, singing, *It's a long way to Tipperary*. 'There's going to be a war,' he yelled. 'You'll be all wanted in the army, you bunch of old crocks.'

We shrank in our stalls, while he walked up and down singing and shouting alternately. His breath smelt very bad and several times he nearly fell; then he went out again singing *Pack up your troubles in your old kit bag*. And we could hear him throwing things about in his house.

'What is a war?' asked Clown.

'A fight,' I answered wishing that Major was still with us because he had known everything. 'I knew a war horse once,' I continued. 'His name was Warrior. He was the only one to come back out of thousands of horses.'

'I couldn't fight,' replied the bay mare. 'I'm too weak.'

'Where did he come back from?' asked Clown.

'From over the sea, in a ship.'

The next day everyone was talking about a war.

Our master felt very ill after so much drink and beat me about the head with a pitch fork. I had a sore on my back from an ill fitting saddle and I felt restless and unhappy.

Three weeks later, the war started and very soon Mr. Smith's hay ran out. There was none coming from Australia or Canada any more, and the fields of England had been allowed to go to waste. Soon there were no oats either. The young men and women joined the army, while we horses grew thinner and thinner. Then one day Mr. Smith came into the stable very drunk. He hit Clown for not moving over quickly and threw a bucket of water over Starlight who laid his ears back at him. Then he reeled from one side of the stable to the other, talking wildly, with sweat running down his face. Then his breath started to come in gasps and he sat down on a truss of hay, his face slowly turning blue. A few more minutes and he was dead.

We all knew death by this time, but for a while

none of us spoke, then the bay mare who had been called Mimosa asked,

'Who will feed us now?'

And Clown said, 'And who will water us?'

'No one,' replied Starlight. 'We will die in our stalls.'

And we, who had hated our master, all wished he would come alive again. The day passed. Our mangers were empty; we had eaten the last wisps of foul smelling hay which had lain in crevices around our mangers for many a long day. The mice ran squeaking around our feet searching out the last few precious spilled oats. The rats looked at us in dismay. Day became night. It was a long uncomfortable night.

'We will die,' said Mimosa, when daybreak came, wrenching against the rope which held her.

I had been there longer than any of the others and I felt very weak; I was the thinnest. Clown pulled on his head collar and neighed. 'No one will hear you,' said Starlight.

'On Saturday our riders will come,' replied Clown.

'We'll be dead by Saturday.'

I could feel my tongue swelling in my mouth. My stall was foul with dung. Clown kicked the walls of his partition. Ponies have a stronger constitution than horses: they can live on less. He would not give up, but kept up a continual neighing and kicking. The doors were closed. We could see nothing but each other and our dead master. The rats came back with the dusk. Finding no food the mice were already leaving. The rats hovered round our legs, waiting for

us to grow weaker, waiting to eat our poor starved flesh. Clown killed two daring ones with his neat pale covered hoofs. Another night passed.

The next day we thought we heard voices, but whoever came went away again without opening the stable door. I was too tired to stand up any more. I lay down on the dirty sawdust in my own dung waiting for death.

Clown had stopped kicking and neighing. I could see the rats' sharp eyes, watching, waiting. I remembered my mother. How happy we had been on the farm together.

Hours passed. Then at last we heard voices. They will go away again, I thought. We are doomed to die along with our master.

Clown found the strength to neigh. We could hear hands trying to open the stable door and a voice said, 'Go on trying. Mr. Smith must be here somewhere.' I didn't move. I was ready to die now. The rats scurried away at the sound of human voices.

Mimosa gave a low whinny deep in her throat. The door opened and two small faces with crash caps on their heads peered in.

'Mr. Smith,' one of them called nervously. 'Mr.

87

Smith, where are you? It's Sally and Chrissy. We've come for our ride.'

They stepped into the stable timidly, like children into an ogre's den, looking round them with frightened eyes. They saw Mr. Smith's body and their mouths fell open with surprise.

'Mr. Smith, Mr. Smith, are you awake?' they called before the smaller one screamed. 'He's dead. Can't you see? He's dead!'

They ran outside again.

'That's that,' said Mimosa.

'They must tell someone,' replied Clown.

We heard them ride away on their bicycles. They had left the door open and fresh air came in like a gift from heaven. The rats scurried out of the door.

'They will send someone,' said Clown with hope in his voice.

We waited; rain was pattering now on the old tin roof. Then at last there were voices, more and more voices, policemen, a doctor, an ambulance. They took our master away on a stretcher and then they looked at us.

'Crickey,' cried one. 'They are like walking corpses.' 'They are only fit for the knackers,' said another.

They fetched us hay and fresh water from the house, such water as we had not tasted in months.

The house was full of police. An old man came and cleaned our stalls. Someone went away and came back with oats, though oats were supposed to be unobtainable just then. The old man groomed us making a hissing noise, reminding us of our younger days. Next day a man of around forty came in uniform. He looked at us in dismay. He ran his hands through our staring coats, and said, 'They're covered with lice. I'll borrow Dad's bike and go down to the farm and see if they've got something to kill them.'

He had fair hair, a round face with a fresh complexion. It was difficult to believe that he was our late master's son.

Later his wife came with their four children. They took everything out of Mr. Smith's house and the wife wept over us.

He only had three days' compassionate leave from the army, but he did his best. He found us food from somewhere and scrubbed our stalls and bedded them in fresh golden straw. He deloused us and wormed us and paid the old man to go on looking after us. Then he went back to his unit.

The old man said, 'No one will want you. They're shooting horses as it is.' He brought a gas mask every day with him and hung it on a nail.

We grew stronger. We were advertised for sale and people came and looked at us, pulled our mouths open, felt our legs and said, 'They're not even fat enough for meat.'

Then Chrissy and Sally came one day with their mother. They kept saying, 'Please, please we must have him. Please, please, please.' They threw their arms round Clown's thin neck and begged. 'We can ride to school,' they said. 'We can buy him a cart, please Mummy please.'

Finally their mother gave the old man ten pounds and they led Clown away.

No one wanted Starlight because of his ring bone, but presently a farmer bought Mimosa to pull his hay cutter.

I was better in body but becoming more and more dejected in spirit. 'If no one comes for you tomorrow it's goodbye old fellow,' said the old man. 'That's my orders. I was to wait a week.'

I had been ready to die but now I felt better. I looked out of the stable door which was open all the time now and smelt spring coming, the sap rising in the trees, the grass pushing its way through the damp earth. I remembered the pleasure of rolling, the taste of dew drenched grass.

I shifted my weight from one leg to another. My strength was coming back.

'A lot more are going to die before this war's finished,' said the old man.

I've heard people say, 'It's always darkest before dawn.' And that is how it was with me. The last day came. Starlight and I looked at each other sadly, wondering which of us would go first.

Then a lady came riding into the yard on a dun mare. She dismounted and called, 'Hoi. Are you in charge? Have you a horse here called Black Velvet?'

'Not that I know of,' replied the old man. 'Though we have got an old black horse inside.'

'He was once a show jumper,' she said. 'A man called Bert told me he was here.'

'I'll hold your mare while you look,' said the old man.

She had short wavy hair and an upturned nose.

She said, 'Poor old chap, so you were once a show

jumper with a mouth like velvet. What a shame.'

'You are only just in time. I have orders to call the horse slaughterers after I've had my dinner,' said the old man through the doorway.

'He's twelve pounds, isn't he? I've brought the money,' she answered, opening her purse.

I wondered why she wanted me as the old man led me out into the daylight, saying, 'You're in luck after all.' And I was sorry for Starlight, for I knew now that he had no future, only the humane killer.

'I'm leading him home,' said my new mistress mounting her mare. 'It's twelve miles. Do you think he will make it?'

'If you take it slowly he will.'

'I promised an old school friend that I would buy him. Her name is Bastable. Her husband was killed last week in France,' she said. 'He's going to live in honourable retirement.'

Starlight neighed. I was sorry to leave him to his fate alone; I wished that he could have come with us. If I could have spoken I would have pleaded for him, begged for his life, as it was I neighed a long sad farewell and hoped that his end would be swift and painless.

CHAPTER ELEVEN

My last home

It was a long way. I grew very tired. We stopped to rest me and once I recognised the landscape and saw that we had halted nearby to where I was born. But everything was changed. The old buildings were falling down with neglect; the hedges had been replaced by sagging barbed wire. The trees under which we had stood on hot summer days were gone and, worst of all, the paddock near the house had houses on it. I felt very sad when I saw the change. The fields were being ploughed by two tractors. A different breed of cow was waiting to be milked.

We went on, my new mistress, who was called Jean, whistling as we went, the dun mare saying, 'Can't you walk any faster? I want to get home.'

I wondered whether Starlight had been shot yet. There were pill boxes [machine-gun positions] at the side of the roads, but not many soldiers to be seen. Then we saw a sandbagged post with a large gun pointing towards the sky. Soon afterwards we turned down a lane and came to an old white cottage with roses climbing up its walls.

Two children and a dog came to greet us. The boy was called Paul, the girl Sonia. They both had fair hair like their mother.

'Gosh, he looks awful,' Sonia said.

'Do you think he's going to live?'

'Yes, if he has the chance.'

'Mummy, I've milked Tiddlywinks,' said Paul.

'And I've fed Jemina,' said Sonia.

It wasn't a smart place. There were no servants. They did everything themselves. But it was a happy house, perhaps the happiest place I had ever known. Every animal had a name and was loved and looked after. If the chickens were ill they were taken indoors to be warm, if the cat had a bad foot it was tenderly bandaged up. Oats were rationed and I and the dun mare, who was called Amelia, did not qualify for a ration, but there was always plenty of sweet smelling home-made hay. The children rode Amelia and were members of the pony club. They spent hours learning stable management from books. They fussed over our food, as though we were invalids.

On wet days they played a gramophone to us to keep us amused. They fought over who should wind it up and tried to decide which record we preferred. Sometimes they dressed us up in their own clothes. The stable was only an old cow shed, but they had made it into two boxes and they were always bedded down in plenty of straw, so we were always warm and comfortable. Gradually the shine came back to my coat; my sides started to fill out, the poverty marks on my quarters grew less pronounced. Amelia was only six. She had never had a bad home. She was fourteen hands high and full of life. She would never believe my stories.

'Humans are not like that,' she would say. 'Humans are lovely.'

'You wouldn't say that if you had belonged to Mr. Smith or Mr. Chambers,' I answered.

'Well I haven't and I don't believe they exist,' she would answer with a snort. 'You wait until you see our master, he's lovely too.'

She would spend hours licking the children's hands, while I stood aloof, too nervous to approach, afraid of a sudden blow.

The days grew warmer and the sky was full of planes. My new master came home one evening exhausted, his face blackened, his eyes crying out for sleep. He said that things were going very badly and that soon the Germans would be coming and that we must be ready and he gave Jean a gun to use on herself and the children if things got bad. Then he bought a cart and a set of harness and he said that one of us must be put to use to help the war effort. Then his leave was over and he disappeared again and Jean and the children sat and cried, and for the next three nights all we heard was gunfire. It made me feel very nervous but Amelia who had never been ill treated was not afraid. She insisted that it was nothing but thunder, but I knew differently for Warrior had told me about war. After that there was gunfire and bombs and great lights wheeling in the sky night after night and no one slept much. Sonia and Paul would go out early in the morning looking for bits of shrapnel, while Jean waited sad-eyed for the post to come.

Everything was in short supply. But Jean never grumbled. She would say, 'We're the lucky ones, because we live in the country and can grow things.'

Then one day we saw planes chasing each other in the sky.

'They are only playing,' said Amelia.

I knew differently of course – I knew that the men inside were trying to kill each other, and I wondered why man is always fighting and killing. Then one of the planes started coming down in a pall of smoke, and Jean and the children came running from the cottage. Soon we could see men like toys dangling from the sky on parachutes and the children started to shout and wave.

Then Jean said in a strange voice, 'They are Germans. Go for help one of you.'

Amelia was tearing round the field by this time, her tail up over her back, snorting like a mustang. Sonia fetched a head collar.

Jean said, 'It will have to be Black Velvet. Can you manage him?'

'I'll try,' replied Paul. It was many months since I had been ridden, but I stood as quietly as I could and pushed my nose into the head collar. Paul jumped on my back off a gate.

The Germans were untangling themselves from their parachutes two fields away.

I turned quickly. Paul gripped me tightly with his small bony knees.

'Be careful. Godspeed,' shouted Jean.

We galloped up the lane and turned left, Paul crouching on my withers like a jockey. I wasn't fit, but I galloped as fast as I could along the tarmac road. Outside a cottage, an old lady stood staring over her gate. 'Have they come? Is it the invasion?' she cried.

'No. They've been shot down,' yelled Paul. We had reached a police house now. Paul slipped off my back and rapped on the door. A policeman came out carrying his helmet.

'A German plane has been shot down,' shouted Paul. 'Some men have landed by our house.' The policeman ran for his bike.

Paul patted my neck. 'You're lovely,' he said. 'Better than Amelia even.'

He rode me slowly back.

By the time we had reached the house the men were being taken away. One had his face bandaged, another had half an arm missing. They looked fine young men. I felt very sad when I saw them. I could see the charred remains of the plane and Sonia stood waving a bit of wing triumphantly. After that the children and Jean started to ride me quietly and then they put me in the cart and soon I was trotting up and down the empty wartime roads to the shop and back.

I was glad to be of some use. Horses can become bored just like humans and I was tired of my retirement.

CHAPTER TWELVE

Bad news

There followed a long hard winter. It was very cold;
sometimes so cold that the children didn't even go to
school. We spent the nights in our warm loose boxes,
but there was nothing but hay to eat and once, for a
few days, only oat straw.

I lost condition again but continued working, pulling the cart, which was more of a farm cart than a
carriage. More than once I heard Jean say,

'I don't know what we would do without old
Velvet.'

The children drove me to near-by woods and came
back with the cart loaded with firewood. It snowed
for days on end. The holly trees were bright with
berries. But at last spring came.

Jean borrowed a harrow and I harrowed the fields.
Summer came and I pulled a hay cutter. One day
Jean came outside with a letter in her hand. The chil-
dren were cutting nettles to make us nettle hay.

Her face looked crumpled and exhausted. She
called: 'Come over here please.' She put her arms

around them and said, 'This has just come.'

'It is about Daddy, isn't it? He's dead,' said Paul. Sonia didn't speak.

'It says he's missing, believed killed,' replied Jean. 'But only believed. They haven't found him.'

'Found him?' asked Sonia.

'His body,' replied Paul.

They stayed close together without speaking and I was very sorry for them. 'The master's dead,' I told Amelia.

'We don't belong to him, we belong to Jean, she feeds us,' Amelia replied.

'Silly ignorant mare,' I retorted, though I am not usually rude. 'He's dead and he was a fine young man and it will affect us all.'

The next day there was much talk of selling the farm and leaving. I knew that if that happened there was no hope for me. I was twenty years old now and very tired. My back was hollow, and old saddle sores had left grey hairs on my back and withers. Lack of oats made me tire easily and, though I did my best, I knew I couldn't work as I had when I was younger.

Jean and the children understood this and let me go at my own pace and, as I always did my best, they never used a whip or stick.

I was worried now. I had been very happy. I had no wish to start again in a new home. Fortunately after much talk, it was decided that Jean and the children should stay where they were to the end of the war.

Jemina died and the children put her body in a black box and put me in the cart and dressed themselves in black. I had to pull her coffin to a small grave by the pond where she was buried. It seemed odd to bury a little duck with such ceremony when so many young men were dying all over the world.

Another winter came. Everyone had become accustomed to our master being dead. Paul tried hard to be the man about the house, chopping the wood and digging the vegetable patch. Sonia rode Amelia most of the time now. She was too silly to pull the cart so she was kept mostly for pleasure, though sometimes she was ridden into the nearby town to do the shopping.

Jean looked very worn. She was trying to make a living out of the land and soon I was carrying vegetables and fruit into the nearby town on market day. Then two cows were bought and more chickens.

Then one night, Paul came running out to the stable with a torch.

'Wake up, Black Velvet, you're needed. Sonia's very ill. And there's no petrol anywhere and the bikes are punctured. You'll have to take her to the doctor in the cart.'

He pushed my head into the collar and threw the rest of the harness over my back. I pushed my head into the bridle. I had been to market once already that day and was tired, but I knew by the urgency in Paul's voice that this was a matter of life or death. He dragged me outside and pushed me between the shafts of the cart. There was a bright moon shining and everything was frozen. Jean came out carrying Sonia wrapped in blankets.

'I'll be all right soon,' said Sonia between chattering teeth. 'If only it didn't hurt. I'm sorry Mummy. I know I'm being a nuisance, but it does hurt.'

'A nuisance? Don't be so silly. You've got an appendicitis and if I hadn't been so busy with the cow calving, and it being market day and everything else, I would have noticed hours ago.'

And with that she put her gently into the cart propped up against the seat with pillows and got up herself, her face very white. Paul jumped in the back.

'Steady. Go gently, Black Velvet,' Jean said.

I did my best. The road was covered with ice. How I stayed on my legs I shall never know. Sonia was moaning all the time and I could hear Paul's voice saying, 'It's going to be all right, Mummy.'

'What do you mean – all right? If her appendix bursts the poison will be all over her body; and it will be my fault if she dies, because I didn't know it was so bad when she complained earlier. I shall have killed her, Paul,' replied Jean.

I heard Sonia say, very quietly, 'No Mummy.' And Paul said:

'She'll be all right. We are going to get there in time.' But I could hear how worried he was and knew he was only trying to comfort his mother.

'Sometimes I think I have had enough,' she went on. 'If your father was coming home, if the farm paid, if anything went right it would be different.'

'You're tired,' Paul answered. 'Tired to death.'

We had reached the Doctor's house. Paul ran to the door and started beating upon it with his fists. Presently a window was opened and a lady said, 'What is it? The doctor's gone to Pickwicks. There's been an explosion. A bomb, I think. There's lots of dead.'

'My daughter has an appendicitis,' shouted Jean. 'It's urgent.'

'There's many dead and injured,' replied the lady shutting the window.

'Let's try another doctor. We can telephone from the kiosk,' Paul said.

He jumped out of the cart and ran up the road, but was soon back saying, 'It doesn't work. The line is dead. We had better drive on to the hospital. We may meet someone. Come on.'

Jean jerked the reins and I set off as fast as I could on the slippery road. Sonia had stopped moaning. Jean kept saying, 'Faster, Black Velvet. Come on. Move on.'

The road was empty. There were houses, but you couldn't see them because their windows were blacked out. We had no lamps at all on the cart. Snow started to fall in small, white flakes.

'I can hear something coming,' shouted Paul. He leapt out of the cart and stood waving in the road.

'Are you going into town? We've got a sick person here. She's dying,' he shouted.

The car stopped. A man leaned out. 'Jump inside,' he shouted.

'Go on, Mummy,' yelled Paul. 'I'll take Black Velvet back.'

The man helped Jean lift Sonia gently into the car. She couldn't move her legs by this time and she was groaning all the time.

'Right you are,' said the man and the car was gone.

'Home,' said Paul, fighting back tears. 'I'll walk with you, Velvet. I'm so cold it may warm me up.'

It was a long cold road home before Paul put me away in the stable. 'I'm sorry there's no mash for you, no oats,' he said, giving me a carrot. 'One day this war will be over and we'll give you a great bucketful of oats, but now I must go in, though I would rather stay with you, for the fire is out and the house is freezing.'

Jean came back the next morning on the bus. She had not slept all night. 'She's not out of danger yet,' she said. 'It burst. I just came back to milk the cows.'

'I can manage, but I would like to see her some-time,' said Paul with a break in his voice. 'Is she going to die?'

'They say so. They say there's no hope.'

The next few days were terrible, even Amelia was affected, because she thought the world of Sonia. We hardly saw Jean, neighbours came and fed us when they could and a strange boy milked the two cows.

Gloom hung over the little farm like a big dark cloud, none of us cared much if we lived or died.

Then one morning Paul came running down to the stable crying, 'She's out of danger; she's going to be all right. She's saved, Velvet – saved.' And he put his arms round my neck and buried his face in my mane.

Then, after some weeks had passed, Sonia came back looking pale and fragile and needing extra food which wasn't there, though there was plenty of milk now because of the cows, and eggs too, and veget-ables, so we were luckier than most people.

The roads were crammed with soldiers now in tanks and armoured vehicles; they came down to the farm for water. There were many Americans and

Canadians. They said they had come to save us from the Germans.

Then suddenly they were all gone and people seemed a little more cheerful and there was talk of when the war was over. But Jean never talked about it though once I heard her say,

'When peace comes I shan't feel like celebrating, because I shall know then that Alan will never come back.'

Sonia grew stronger. Paul grew taller and we could all see that soon he would be a man. And then suddenly part of the war was over and people lit great bonfires and danced and there was much singing.

Jean stayed inside with the children without saying much, though a few days later she said, 'We will have to sort out our future soon. We can't go on here. It's too isolated for just us three, and what shall I do, Paul, when you go away? When you are grown up?'

'I'll stay with you, Mummy,' Sonia said. 'And there's always the horses.' But Jean was determined to go now. 'You need friends,' she told the children, 'and you will never make friends here. You'll want to go to dances.'

Then the rest of the war ended and the church bells rang, and all the houses were lit up again, and then the soldiers started to come home.

Everyone was much merrier in the village and there was talk of more food soon.

Jean decided to sell the farm. 'I want to be near to relations,' she said. 'I can't stand the loneliness any more. We can find Amelia a nice home; but Velvet will have to be put down.'

We were all older. Sonia and Paul were fifteen and I was well past twenty. I stood under the trees a lot now remembering the past. I had seen many changes. I had lived through a fearful war. I had seen the emergence of a new style of riding. I had witnessed horses being driven from the farms by tractors and watched them come back in wartime. I was content to go peacefully. I had been very happy on the farm. I was grateful for the years there.

A notice was nailed up at the front of the house saying FOR SALE. The children cried. The cows were sold. Amelia grew anxious now. I wanted to give her good advice but she would not listen.

'You are too old,' she said. 'You don't know anything. Times have changed.'

'But human nature hasn't. There will always be good and bad masters,' I said.

'Masters, Mistresses! We call them our owners, nowadays,' she retorted. 'I shall teach my next one a thing or two, I can tell you.'

People came to look over the house, complaining that there was no telephone and only one bathroom, and no central heating, just as they had complained over Matthew's cottage all those years ago.

Then one day a tall gaunt man in uniform came walking up the path. One of his sleeves was empty and his hair was grey. He looked at the notice before he knocked on the back door. Jean came out her hands dirty from cleaning the grate. 'I see this place is for sale,' he said. 'Oh, Jean!'

She stared at him and said, 'Alan! It can't be.' But she kept staring at him.

Amelia and I watched without speaking.

'I built a railway. I was in prison a long time. But I'm Alan, all right, minus one arm, of course,' he said.

'It doesn't matter.'

'How pleased the children will be. They're at school,' gasped Jean.

'Oh Alan, I thought I would never see you again!'

'The thought of this place and you, kept me alive. Let's take down the notice, we're not leaving,' he said, stooping to kiss her. She started to cry. 'I'm so happy,' she said.

They fetched a hammer and took down the notice. 'I was going to sell everything. The cows have gone already,' Jean told him.

'Not any more,' said Alan, his one arm round her.

They talked for a long time. He had been sent to Australia because he was like a scarecrow. 'They fattened me up there,' he said. 'You should have had a letter. Something went wrong.'

'It doesn't matter now,' she said. 'I was going to have Black Velvet put down and sell Amelia, but they can stay now, can't they? Black Velvet saved Sonia's life, you know. No other horse could have stood up on the roads that night. They were covered with ice. I think he knew how ill she was . . . I never stopped hoping you would come back. Not until the war was over. I couldn't celebrate then,' she said.

'We'll have our own celebration this evening,' he promised.

Sonia and Paul came home later and a great bonfire was lit in the paddock. Amelia and I watched as they danced round it singing old war songs. I felt very tired but happy too for I knew now that this was my home for ever. Amelia pranced up and down snorting at the flames, but I wasn't afraid because I knew I would never be hurt again.

Later they said good night to us.

'You really are going to be pensioned off this time,' Sonia told me one arm round my neck. 'You are going to live here to the end of your days and, when your time comes, you will be buried under the apple trees with a gravestone with *Black Velvet* on it, for all to see.'

I remembered how Mouse and Twilight had died, and poor Starlight killed because of ringbone. They had all been quite young. I was old now. Soon I would be ready to go wherever horses go. Perhaps I would meet my mother there and all the other horses I had known – my own generation. They would be sound and young again and we would talk about the old days, not about owners and the pony club, but about masters and mistresses and carriages and phaetons, about the days when tails were still docked and we pulled the carts and ploughs of England.

If you've enjoyed reading this book, why don't you try some of the other stories about horses and riding available in Knight Books? Here and on the pages following are some of our suggestions:

Helen Griffiths

STALLION OF THE SANDS

The beautiful wild albino stallion who roamed the fog-bound Atlantic shores had become a legend to the gauchos, a ghost-horse. Yet Aurelio, the orphan boy who had joined the tough gaucho band, was determined to find the horse – and to tame him. It was said that the one who succeeded in capturing and riding the sand stallion would be the most 'gaucho' of them all, and for Aurelio, recently dishonoured in the eyes of the band, it was a challenge too strong to resist.

KNIGHT BOOKS

Patricia Leitch

CROSS-COUNTRY PONY

Jinty and Nick decide to spend their summer holidays organising a pets' home, and their first resident is the pony Harold. Harold is ugly and has the habit of bucking. By accident Jinty discovers he is a marvellous jumper and cross-country galloper, but in the local show Harold lets Jinty down in the games and the jumping. Jinty and Nick have other troublesome and exciting residents at their pets' holiday home in this thrilling story.

A PONY OF OUR OWN

'We're a standing joke with everyone: "The Donaldsons, who are desperate to ride, haven't a horse, and when they do manage to borrow one, are too feeble to stay on." '

But perhaps the jokes would stop now, for at last Jean and her brother Stuart had saved up enough to buy a pony of their own. Jean dreamed of a neat grey or a dashing bay hunter.

But as it turned out, she was quite wrong.

KNIGHT BOOKS

Anna Sewell
☐ 17428 5   BLACK BEAUTY   50p

Josephine Pullein-Thompson
☐ 23237 4   BLACK EBONY   60p

Diana Pullein-Thompson
☐ 23238 2   BLACK PRINCESS   60p

Helen Griffiths
☐ 21383 3   STALLION OF THE SANDS   65p

Judith Berrisford
☐ 19526 6   A PONY IN THE FAMILY   60p
☐ 21658 1   A COLT IN THE FAMILY   60p
☐ 21657 3   A SHOW JUMPER IN THE
FAMILY   60p

Patricia Leitch
☐ 19165 1   CROSS-COUNTRY PONY   60p
☐ 03757 1   A PONY OF OUR OWN   60p

All these books are available at your local bookshop or newsagent, or can be ordered direct from the publisher. Just tick the titles you want and fill in the form below.

Prices and availability subject to change without notice.

KNIGHT BOOKS, P.O. Box 11, Falmouth, Cornwall.

Please send cheque or postal order, and allow the following for postage and packing:

U.K.—One book 19p plus 9p per copy for each additional book ordered, up to a maximum of 73p.

B.F.P.O. and EIRE—19p for the first book plus 9p per copy for the next 6 books, thereafter 3p per book.

OTHER OVERSEAS CUSTOMERS—20p for the first book and 10p per copy for each additional book.

Name ....

Adress ....

....